8 Year Old Girls Are Fantastic

A Collection of Wonderful Stories for Girls
Sparking Self-Love, Confidence, Mindfulness,
and Big Dreams (Inspirational Books for Kids)

Table of Contents

Introduction

Hello, dear girl,

Welcome to a book that is as special and unique as you are! Within these pages lie stories of brave hearts, endless dreams, and the gentle whisper of courage that tells us we can achieve anything we set our hearts on.

Every girl holds a sprinkle of magic within her, a kind of magic that grows brighter with every challenge faced and every fear chased away. This book is full of such magical stories that will take you on a journey to faraway places and close-to-home adventures.

As you dance through these pages, you will meet many hearts who faced their fears, shared giggles with their friends, and discovered the delightful truth that they are capable of creating wonders. And guess what? They are just like you, with dreams in their eyes and a bundle of hopes wrapped tightly in their hearts.

These tales will take you on a rollercoaster of adventures where the skies are painted with bravery, the winds hum tunes of self-love, and the flowers bloom with self-confidence. They remind us that every little step we take, no matter how wobbly, is a dance move in the grand ballet of life. And every time we dare to dance to our own tune, we spread sparkles of inspiration for everyone around.

Dear girl, as you read each story, imagine yourself as a brave adventurer, an unstoppable dreamer, and a kind-hearted friend. Feel the flutter of magic wings around you, ready to take you to lands where dreams grow on trees and courage blooms in every heart.

Are you ready to dive into the whirlpool of adventures and discover the magic that you hold within? Here we go, on a journey where each story is a friend waiting to hold your hand and twirl with you in the dance of life.

With sparkles of love and pages filled with dreams, your companions in this magical journey.

"The Tiny Knight"

Once upon a time, in a small town, there lived a sweet 8-year-old girl named Emma. Emma was known for her soft voice and gentle heart. She had a magical way of seeing the good in every situation. However,

Emma was rather timid and the idea of confronting anyone scared her to her core.

Emma attended the local elementary school, where she enjoyed learning new things every day. However, there was a shadow that lingered over her joyful learning experience. A group of bullies at school often picked on her, and others who were soft-spoken like her. They would mock, tease, and sometimes take away her lunch. Emma felt helpless and scared, but didn't know what to do about it.

One fine morning, as Emma was watering the flowers in her little garden, she saw a bird courageously defending its nest from a menacing cat. The small bird, undeterred by the cat's size, chirped loudly and fluttered its wings, shooing the cat away. Emma was awestruck by the tiny bird's bravery. It

sparked something within her—a tiny ember of courage started to flicker.

Days rolled by and the ember of courage within Emma grew stronger. She often watched a bird defending its nest from other birds and sometimes from the cat. In those moments she stood in front of the mirror, rehearsing how she would stand up to the bullies. And then the day came when she could no longer bear to see her friends being bullied. With a shaky breath but firm resolve, Emma approached the bullies as they were mocking a friend of hers.

With a firm yet gentle voice, she said, "It's not right what you're doing. Everyone deserves respect and kindness, not ridicule."

The bullies were taken aback by Emma's sudden spurt of courage. They mumbled and grumbled but eventually walked away, leaving Emma's friend in peace.

As Emma bravely confronted the bullies that day, a change rippled through the school. The bullies, who had never been stood up to before, found themselves at a loss for words. They were taken aback by Emma's audacity, but more than that, they were hit by the truth in her words. The crowd that had gathered around witnessed the soft-spoken Emma show a strength that was quiet yet unyielding. Whispers of admiration swirled through the gathering.

Later that day, the principal of the school, having heard of the confrontation, called the bullies to his office. He had a long talk with

them about the importance of kindness, respect, and the consequences of bullying. The bullies were made to understand the pain they had inflicted upon Emma and other students.

Word spread through the school, and Emma's small act of courage became a subject of many conversations. Emma realized that it was crucial to overcome fears when standing up for what you believe in. She felt a new understanding of the difference one voice could make.

The ripple effect of Emma's bravery was subtle but significant. Some of her classmates, inspired by her act, started to speak up little by little against any unfair treatment. Not everyone, and not always, but it was a start. Emma's simple act of standing

up to the bullies had planted seeds of bravery in the hearts of some of the kids around her.

Emma's story was no fairytale of overnight transformation, but a realistic narrative of slow, steady change and the importance of standing up for what is right, no matter how small the act. It was a quiet reminder to the students—and even the teachers—about the power of courage and the change it can instigate, one small step at a time.

And thus, Emma's tale, rooted in reality, continued to inspire her little world, echoing the profound truth that every act of courage, no matter how small, contributes to a larger change. And with each day, Emma, along with others, strived to create an environment of respect, kindness, and

understanding, nurturing the slowly changing ethos of their small school in the quaint town.

This story highlights the importance of being brave and standing up for what is right, showing that even small acts of courage can create big changes. It encourages facing fears and supporting others to foster a kinder, more respectful environment for everyone.

"Patience Blooms"

In a humble town named Whispering
Willow, known for its serene river and
blossoming trees, lived a young, spirited girl
named Olivia. This town was a close-knit
community where everyone knew everyone

else. The quiet ripples of the river seemed to whisper secrets to the townspeople, binding them in a gentle calm. Olivia lived in a quaint little house with her loving mother, Martha, who was a homemaker and a phenomenal gardener. There was also her doting father, Alfred, who was a skilled carpenter, and a bundle of endless energy, Timmy—her little brother.

Olivia was known for her zest for life and her constant eagerness to learn and grow. She had a curious mind brimming with questions and her eyes sparkled with wonder. However, patience was a virtue she found hard to grasp. Her impulsive nature often saw her jumping from one interest to another, seeking instant gratification.

One fine Sunday morning, as the sun's golden rays cast a warm glow on the roses in their garden, Olivia was captivated by the beauty of a violin's melody that echoed from the neighborhood. The soothing tune played by old Mrs. Brunner, a violin teacher, from down the lane, filled the air with magic. Olivia, enchanted, decided she too wanted to play the violin.

With her parents' supportive nod, Olivia found herself knocking on Mrs. Brunner's door the very next day. As Mrs. Brunner welcomed her in, she cautioned Olivia about the patience and perseverance required to master the violin. Yet, the caution floated away on the strings of enthusiasm as Olivia held the violin in her arms.

The first week saw Olivia bubbling with enthusiasm. The hours she spent with Mrs. Brunner were filled with basic lessons and endless attempts to play a simple tune. But as the days went by, Olivia's excitement began to wane. The violin didn't sing like it did in Mrs. Brunner's hands; instead, it screeched and wailed. Her fingers ached, and the initial magic seemed to vanish in the face of reality. Olivia's friends, noticing her struggle, would often invite her to play by the river, their laughter ringing a tempting tune.

Her mother's gentle words on a quiet evening resonated through her thoughts. "Honey, beautiful things take time and patience." Yet, Olivia was on the verge of giving up.

One cloudy morning, after another failed attempt to play a simple tune, the melancholy within Olivia reached new heights. Each screech of the violin seemed to mock her inability. The room which had once resonated with her enthusiasm now echoed with the gnawing silence of disappointment. Mrs. Brunner found Olivia on the brink of tears, clutching the violin as though it were a fragment of her shattered dreams.

Mrs. Brunner sat down beside Olivia, her eyes filled with a tender understanding that only years of experience could bring. With a comforting hand on Olivia's shoulder, she began to share her story. "Olivia, dear, I know this journey seems incredibly tough right now, but let me share a chapter from

my life with you." Mrs. Brunner's voice was a soft contrast to the storm brewing within Olivia.

"There was a time, many moons ago, when I was passionate, eager, but impatient. I remember the day I was introduced to the violin. Oh, it was love at first string. But as days turned into nights and nights into days, my struggle with patience muffled the music within me. There were days I'd cry, feeling the gap between my dreams and reality expand. My fingers ached. My heart ached even more.

"But one day my teacher sat me down under the old willow tree, just like we are sitting now. She told me, 'Patience, dear Brunner, is like a magical note. It's the pause between the chords, the silence between the notes,

16

which makes the melody profound. You've got to allow the music to seep into your soul, allow the rhythm of patience to guide your fingers.' It wasn't the most comforting thing to hear then, but it was the truth.

"The next morning, I woke up with a serene calmness within. I held the violin, not as a challenge but as a companion on a beautiful journey. And every day, every struggle became a note in my melody of patience. It was a slow, tender journey, but a rewarding one indeed."

Mrs. Brunner's words painted hope in the bleak landscape of Olivia's heart. It was not just about playing a tune flawlessly; it was about embracing the rhythm of patience, allowing it to mold her into a true musician.

With a renewed resolve, Olivia wiped away her tears, ready to step into the soothing rhythm of patience, one note at a time. Mrs. Brunner's comforting smile was the dawn of a new hope.

Every morning, before the town awoke, the gentle chords of Olivia's new attempts whispered through the calm. Each day, she pushed forward, the sweet melody of patience slowly tuning her heart and hands. Her friends stood by, their encouragement a soft melody.

The season of patience bore fruit on a sunny morning when Olivia played her first tune flawlessly. The magic resonated through every heart in Whispering Willow, as the sweet melody of success—the virtue of

patience now a part of Olivia's soul—danced through the lanes.

As days blossomed into nights, Olivia's music became a soulful part of the community. Her parents' hearts swelled with pride, Timmy looked up to his sister with awe, and her friends found inspiration in her journey.

And on a beautiful evening by the river, with the whole town gathered, Olivia played the melody of perseverance and patience. The tale of a young girl's journey echoed through Whispering Willow, inspiring many. A melody of dedication now intertwined with the whispers of the calm river, narrating the tale of little Olivia's blooming patience.

This story highlights the importance of patience and practice to get better at something, even when it gets tough. Through Olivia's story, we learn that good things take time, and support from family and friends makes the journey easier and worthwhile.

"The Melody of Courage"

In a quaint and beautiful little town lived a
tender-hearted 8-year-old girl named
Amelia. Amelia was known for her
melodious hums that often accompanied her
during her daily chores. However, she only

sang to the flowers in her garden, the stars in the night sky, and the walls of her cozy room. The thought of singing in front of others sent shivers down her spine.

The announcement of the annual talent show at her school sent a ripple of excitement among the students. Amelia's friends, who had often heard the sweet whispers of her tunes, urged her to share her gift on the stage. The very thought of standing on the stage, under the bright lights, with countless eyes upon her, made Amelia's stomach churn. However, her heart fluttered at the idea of filling the room with her melodies.

With hesitant hope, Amelia decided to start by singing in front of her family. As she

stood in her living room, facing her parents and her older brother, her throat seemed to close up. The words of the song that she knew by heart scattered with her fleeing courage. Though her family cheered her on, Amelia couldn't go past the first line of the song. She felt a deep sense of disappointment, but a small voice within nudged her to keep trying.

Her next attempt was at a small gathering in her backyard with a few close friends. Though the familiar faces were comforting, her voice quivered with fear. Her friends cheered and encouraged her. Their love and support were heartening, yet the shackles of stage fright were too tight.

The days rolled by, and the date of the talent show loomed closer. The waves of courage and fear danced within Amelia, making her heart race with conflicting emotions. Her little heart wanted so badly to share her love for singing, to feel the joy that her melodies brought to her, with everyone else.

The morning of the talent show arrived, bringing along a sky filled with butterflies fluttering wildly in Amelia's stomach. As she stood backstage, waiting for her turn, she felt her legs tremble. However, she remembered her family's comforting smiles, her friends' encouraging cheers, and the beautiful birds that sang fearlessly.

Amelia stepped onto the stage, the spotlight casting a warm glow on her face. She looked

at the audience, took a deep breath, closed her eyes, and allowed her love for singing to guide her. The first note was soft, almost a whisper, her fear trying to grip her. But with each passing note, her fear melted away, making way for a stream of beautiful, confident melodies that danced through the room, touching every heart.

The hall erupted in applause as Amelia hit the final note. Her eyes twinkled with the joy of overcoming her fears and the satisfaction of a dream realized. She took a bow, her heart filled with a melody of courage that sang louder than her fears. The cheers and claps resonated through the hall, echoing her achievement not only to her but to everyone present.

As she stepped off the stage, her friends rushed to her, their faces bright with pride and excitement. They surrounded her with hugs and words of admiration. Her family, standing a little farther away, had tears of joy gleaming in their eyes. They came forward and enveloped her in a warm, comforting hug, whispering words of love and pride into her ears. They understood as no other that her story wasn't about the overnight conquering of fear, but a testament to the gentle process of facing and overcoming one's fears, one small step at a time.

Amelia's tale exemplifies that overcoming fears, especially the ones that stand between us and our passions, might require small steps, gentle tries, and unwavering support from our loved ones.

Each small attempt, each ounce of encouragement, brings us closer to breaking free from the chains of fear, propelling us towards the path of self-confidence and joy.

"The Loveable Loner"

Once upon a time, in the quaint, picturesque town of Rosewood, lived a gentle soul named Ruby. The town was a palette of warm colors with tiny cottages nestled close to one another, and every dawn brought

with it a fresh, sweet scent of blooming roses, which is how Rosewood got its name. The residents of Rosewood were known for their welcoming nature and hearty laughter that resonated through the peaceful lanes. Yet among this lively populace, Ruby was known for her tranquil spirit.

Ruby had a deep affinity for solitude and the myriad joys it brought to her little heart. She lived in a cozy home that sat beside a beautiful garden, filled with wildflowers of every hue and butterflies that danced in the morning sun. The home housed her small, loving family—her thoughtful mother, Laura, who was a baker, her gentle father, Edward, who was a writer, and a playful little dog named Sprinkles, who was her joyful companion in solitude.

Ruby was often found lost in her dreamy world, nestled among the flowers, whispering secrets to the butterflies, or simply lying on the grass, watching the clouds morph into magical shapes. She enjoyed the quiet. Her parents were understanding and cherished the depth of her serene nature. They respected her love for solitude, seeing a reflection of her father's contemplative disposition in her. However, deep down, they also wished for Ruby to experience the bubbling joy of friendships and the warmth of shared laughter.

The townsfolk were kind-hearted, and the children vibrant and playful, yet Ruby found her calm in the silent conversations with nature and her imaginative explorations. The

first call of change came on a bright Monday morning when her school teacher, Mrs. Anderson, assigned a group project. Ruby was grouped with lively Ella and creative Liam. They were thrilled, but Ruby felt a sudden rain cloud looming over her head.

Her usual serene afternoons were replaced with brainstorming sessions. The playful banter between Ella and Liam sounded like an unfamiliar tune to Ruby. She longed for her peaceful corner beside the window where her imagination flowed like a free river. Now, the river seemed to stumble upon rocks of forced conversation and unfamiliar faces.

With a heart full of mixed emotions, Ruby decided to brave the unfamiliar waters of

social interaction. Each day became a blend of awkward conversations, surprising laughter, and growing warmth between her, Ella, and Liam. They navigated through the days, working on their project, sometimes stumbling but helping each other along the way.

One particular sunny afternoon brought with it a revelation that etched into Ruby's heart. The trio decided to work in Ruby's cherished garden, under the shade of the old oak tree. As they sat there amidst the blooms, ideas flowed, laughter echoed, and for the first time, Ruby found the noise comforting.

The hours ticked away unnoticed as they shared tales, cookies baked by Ruby's

mother, and their little dreams. The scene was simple, yet filled with a warm, glowing aura of companionship. Ruby shared her dream of painting a giant mural someday, Ella spoke about her love for animals, and Liam shared his quirky wish to invent a cloud-catching machine. They laughed, they dreamed together, and the world seemed a little more colorful.

As the sun cast long shadows, painting the garden in golden hues, Ruby felt a sweet happiness curling around her heart. She watched Ella and Liam chase Sprinkles around the garden, their laughter mingling with the gentle rustle of leaves. It was different; it was heartwarming. The giggles filled the spaces between the trees, adding a melody to the quiet. Ruby joined in the

laughter, and the echoing joy created a new kind of beauty, one that Ruby had never imagined before.

Her parents, watching from the porch, had smiles reaching their eyes, witnessing the blossoming friendships and the joy it brought to their daughter's eyes. When the dusk draped around, and Ella and Liam bid goodbye with promises to return, Ruby sat by the window, the sky painting shades of twilight. She was reflecting on this recent turn of events, a gentle smile playing on her lips. Her world of solitude was still there, still as enriching, but now she had discovered another world, where shared laughter and companionship had its own charm, its own color.

As days bloomed into shared experiences and playful afternoons, Ruby's world expanded. She continued cherishing her mornings of solitude, where her creativity bloomed, and started appreciating the afternoons of friendship, where her heart laughed. The harmonious blend enriched not just her world but left a gentle, warm breeze of understanding in the community about the essence of a balanced life, and how it should be filled with self-reflection and shared laughter.

The story of Ruby underlines the beauty and necessity of balance between solitude and social interaction in one's life. It teaches that while solitude nurtures creativity and self-reflection, companionship brings about shared laughter, experiences, and a different color to life. Through

embracing both aspects, we not only enrich our own lives, but also contribute to a harmonious understanding within the community, fostering a well-rounded and fulfilling existence.

"Finding Calm in the Chaos"

Jasmine lived in Brightsville, a bustling town always alive with activity. Whether it was the honks of the buses or kids playing in the park, there was never a quiet moment. In a comfortable apartment on Main Street,

Jasmine lived with her mom, dad, younger brother Max, and their parrot, Echo.

Jasmine was a bubbly 8-year-old with bouncy curly hair and freckles sprinkled across her nose. She was always on the go, from school projects to soccer practice to dance lessons. She loved the busy life but sometimes felt overwhelmed juggling everything.

One particular week was super hectic for Jasmine. She had a big math test, a dance recital, and soccer finals. She started forgetting her homework, misplacing her dance shoes, and even missed a soccer practice. It felt like her mind was a browser with 100 tabs open. One day, after forgetting

her lunch at home, Jasmine broke down in tears in front of her teacher, Ms. Lynn.

Ms. Lynn, a gentle lady with silver hair and soft eyes, took Jasmine aside. "It seems like you have a whirlwind inside you," she observed. Jasmine nodded, sniffling. She felt she was letting everyone down: Her team, her dance group, herself.

Ms. Lynn kindly hugged her and shared a story of how she'd felt the same when she was younger. She introduced Jasmine to the world of mindfulness, explaining it as "a way to calm the storm inside and be in the present moment" and invited her to a mindfulness workshop for kids.

Always curious, Jasmine decided to attend the workshop that weekend. The room was

filled with soft cushions, gentle music, and a calming scent. Ms. Maya, the leader of the workshop, taught Jasmine and the other kids about deep breathing, feeling their heartbeat, and focusing on the 'now.' She explained how it was okay to feel overwhelmed, but by being kind to oneself and practicing mindfulness, they could find peace.

Jasmine began practicing mindfulness every day. When she felt stressed, she'd take deep breaths and focus on the moment. Step by step, she started being kinder to herself, understanding it was okay to ask for help or take breaks. The biggest change? She became more organized and less forgetful.

Her family noticed the difference too. Inspired by her, her parents started a

'Mindful Minute' every evening, where they'd sit together, breathe deeply, and share their feelings. Jasmine's friends saw how much calmer she was and wanted in on the secret. So, Jasmine and Ms. Lynn started a little mindfulness club at school. It became a hit!

Jasmine's journey into mindfulness had a ripple effect. Jasmine's story taught other kids an important lesson: In the chaos of life, taking a moment to breathe, be present, and be kind to oneself can make all the difference.

This story imparts a valuable lesson on the importance of mindfulness and self-compassion amid the bustling demands of daily life. Through Jasmine's experience, it's emphasized that adopting practices like mindfulness not only helps in

managing stress but also improves one's overall organization and efficiency. Moreover, by embracing and sharing coping mechanisms, we can foster a community of understanding and support, thus creating a positive ripple effect in the lives of others.

"The Rainbow Connection"

In a quaint little town lived an imaginative girl named Lily. Lily was always curious, filled with questions about the world around her. She had a close-knit group of friends who shared similar interests and backgrounds.

One sunny morning, a new girl named Amina joined Lily's class. Amina had recently moved from a faraway land and brought with her tales and traditions unfamiliar to the folks of the quaint town. She wore colorful headscarves, spoke with a beautiful accent, and shared stories of lands that seemed magical to Lily.

Though curious, Lily hesitated to approach Amina due to their apparent differences. She wasn't sure if they would have anything in common. However, fate brought them together as partners for a school project about traditions around the world. The pairing was unexpected, and Lily felt a mixture of apprehension and excitement.

As they sat down together to discuss the project, they decided to delve into the fascinating contrasts and similarities between their cultures. Their project was titled "A Tapestry of Traditions," aiming to create a full representation of different cultural practices.

Amina shared tales about her homeland, which was filled with a rich history, vibrant

traditions, and festivities that were vastly different from any Lily had ever known. She told stories of grand celebrations, where families gathered to share joy, gratitude, and delicious feasts. Amina even brought some traditional clothing, ornate with beautiful patterns and colors, and a collection of aromatic spices that added flavor to her family's dishes. The beauty and richness of Amina's heritage were like pages from an enchanting book coming to life right before Lily's eyes.

Lily, in return, shared the homely and cherished traditions of Thanksgiving and Christmas, explaining the importance of family gatherings, the joy of giving, and the serene beauty of the winter season. Together, they discovered that despite the

differences in their cultural practices, the essence of family, love, and community was a common thread that tied their worlds together.

However, as their friendship blossomed and their project took a beautiful shape, not everyone in their class was appreciative of the growing cultural exchange. Some classmates were unable to understand or accept the unfamiliar customs and attire that Amina introduced. They found her accent funny, and her headscarves peculiar. Whispers turned into snickers and soon enough, snide remarks were thrown in Amina's direction.

The critical comments mostly stemmed from ignorance and a lack of exposure to cultures

outside their small community. They found comfort in the familiar and saw Amina's differences as oddities rather than something to learn from and appreciate.

Lily was disheartened to see her friend being subjected to ridicule. She realized that it was not just about completing a school project anymore, but about fostering a culture of acceptance and learning among her peers. She knew it was essential to stand by Amina; to help her classmates see the beauty in embracing diversity—the same beauty that had enriched her own understanding of the world.

Their presentation was a masterpiece of colors, stories, and traditions blending seamlessly, painting a picture of a world

larger and more beautiful than what their classmates had known.

The hall echoed with applause as they concluded, but what mattered most were the faces of wonder and the spark of curiosity among their peers. In the days that followed, conversations began to change. The once mocking classmates now approached Amina with questions, keen to learn more about her background. They started to share their own stories too, discovering a newfound respect for the tapestry of cultures that made up their class.

The project became a cornerstone of learning, not just about different traditions but also about the value of acceptance and the enriching experiences that a diverse

friendship could bring. Lily and Amina had ignited a flame of understanding and empathy that, slowly but surely, began to dissolve the walls of ignorance, making room for a garden of friendship and respect to bloom among the young hearts. Their tale was a testament to the power of acceptance, showing that, with an open heart, the world was indeed a colorful place waiting to be explored, one friendship at a time.

Through the tale of Lily and Amina, young readers can explore the essence of acceptance, the beauty of diverse cultures, and the endless possibilities that friendships can unfold, nurturing the values of self-love, self-confidence, and a wholesome appreciation for the world's splendid diversity.

"The Little Leader"

Once upon a time, in the heart of a peaceful community, there lived a vibrant 8-year-old girl named Sarah. Sarah was known for her cheerful nature and a heart full of dreams. One sunny morning, the community council

announced a project to beautify the local park, inviting volunteers to join hands in creating a colorful garden and a new playground for children.

Sarah was thrilled and eagerly volunteered. To her surprise, she was chosen as the young leader for the children's team due to her enthusiasm and previous little garden projects at home. The responsibility was big, but her heart was bigger, and Sarah accepted the role with a fluttering heart filled with dreams of vibrant flowers and joyful laughter filling the air.

With a cute little badge that read 'Young Leader,' Sarah began her journey. Her team consisted of kids from her neighborhood. Together, they were to plant flowers, paint

benches, and create a mural wall that would tell stories of their community's unity and love.

As the newly minted young leader, Sarah was a whirlpool of enthusiasm. The first team meeting was a kaleidoscope of suggestions, each child buzzing with ideas for the garden and mural. The excitement was palpable, but the meeting soon turned into a cacophony with everyone speaking at the same time.

Sarah felt a little overwhelmed. She wanted to make sure everyone was heard, but how? She then remembered how her teacher would conduct class discussions, by giving each student a chance to speak in turn. Sarah decided to borrow this method.

At their next meeting, she brought a small bell. She explained that they would go around the circle, and each member would get to share their ideas one by one. To signify the change in speaker, she would ring the bell. Everyone agreed to this new system, albeit with a sprinkle of giggles.

The bell worked wonders! Each member patiently waited for their turn and shared their ideas when the bell rang for them.

However, not all ideas could be implemented. Mia, a soft-spoken girl with a love for nature, suggested creating birdhouses and butterfly gardens to attract local wildlife. Benny, who was always energetic, proposed building a small zipline for an adventurous play experience. Leo, a

thoughtful and artistic soul, wanted a sculpted fountain in the middle of the garden, which would tell a story through its design.

Sarah appreciated the creativity behind each idea, however, she also realized the challenges. While the birdhouses and butterfly gardens were a great idea, the maintenance would be a long-term commitment that needed adult supervision. The zipline idea brought a sparkle to every child's eye, but safety concerns and budget constraints came with it. Leo's idea of a sculpted fountain was magnificent but beyond their current resources and skills. Through discussions, Sarah and her team learned to face the reality of practical limitations. They discovered that not every

idea could be brought to life, but each suggestion was a stepping stone toward creating something beautiful and meaningful together.

Lots of other ideas, however, could be easily implemented. Together, they combined some and modified others. It was a process of learning, of compromise, and of understanding the practicalities while keeping the creative spirit alive.

Trying to keep everyone heard, Sarah encouraged her team to vote on crucial decisions, fostering a sense of democracy and collective agreement. The value of every opinion and collaboration helped them to find solutions that reflected a piece of everyone's imagination.

Slowly, the team started to understand the essence of teamwork. They became more open to different ideas, more willing to adjust, and more creative in finding solutions that catered to the essence of what they all envisioned for the community garden and mural.

With each passing day, Sarah was not just leading; she was growing, learning, and evolving with her team. She realized that leadership was about bringing out the best in others, about creating a harmonious melody from the various tunes of thought, and about walking together towards a shared dream.

Weeks passed, and the park started to transform. The once dull and abandoned

place now burst with colors, laughter, and life. The community was astonished by the transformation and especially proud of the young minds who had worked tirelessly to bring the vision to life.

On a bright Saturday morning, the community organized a small celebration to honor the efforts of all volunteers. The park was teeming with happiness, the air filled with the sweet scent of blooming flowers, and the mural stood as a testament to the town's unity and creativity. Sarah, with her 'Young Leader' badge shining bright, stood hand in hand with her team, their faces gleaming with joy and pride.

The Mayor of the town presented Sarah and her team with certificates of appreciation,

praising their determination, teamwork, and the leadership qualities that young Sarah had exhibited. It wasn't just a beautiful park that the community had gained; it was a valuable lesson in teamwork, responsibility, and the boundless potential of young minds when driven by a noble cause.

Through this journey, young readers can see the importance of teamwork and leadership. They can see the beauty of working together and how being open to different ideas helps everyone grow. Solving problems practically, respecting others, and creating a friendly space where all members can share their ideas and grow together—this is what it means to be a leader.

"The Girl Who Dared to Dream"

Once upon a time, in a quaint little town, lived a girl named Ada. Ada had a dream as boundless as the night sky—she wanted to become a scientist. The cosmos fascinated

her; the twinkling stars whispered secrets, and the silvery moon was her companion in endless nights of curiosity. However, the town she lived in had expectations as rigid as old oak trees. Girls in her town were expected to follow traditional paths, and dreams of exploring the unknown realms of science were looked upon as whimsical fantasies.

Despite the stagnant whispers of conformity, Ada's imagination soared through galaxies.

Her pursuit of her dream was a beautiful blend of curiosity and simple endeavors. Each morning, before school, Ada would spend time leafing through colorful science books filled with pictures, which her parents had gathered from the local library. The

images of planets, stars, and Earth's magnificent landscapes ignited sparks of wonder in her eyes.

After school, her backyard became her little exploration zone. With her parents' supervision, she'd inspect the plants, watch the birds, and observe the way small insects moved. Her humble 'lab' was a small table where she kept a magnifying glass to inspect leaves, flowers and, occasionally, a friendly bug who decided to stop by.

The weekend was a time for special projects with her parents. They'd create baking soda and vinegar volcanoes, watch documentaries about the planets, or visit the local science museum where Ada could see and learn about different wonders of the natural

world. Each new piece of information was a treasure, and Ada kept a little notebook where she'd draw what she learned, creating her own encyclopedia of wonders.

Her parents also helped her join a weekend science club for kids in a nearby town, where Ada met other young aspiring scientists. They would engage in simple experiments, learn about the basics of science, and share their dreams of what area of science they were most excited to explore as they grew older.

Occasionally, her school would host small science fairs where older students would showcase their projects. Ada would wander around with wide-eyed wonder, asking questions, and imagining what kind of

projects she might work on when she was older.

Every night before bed, Ada would gaze out of her window at the stars, her heart filled with dreams that stretched as far and wide as the cosmos she was so enchanted by. Each day, with the love and support of her parents, she took small, joyful steps towards her dream, cultivating a love for learning and a belief in the magic of science.

Though her zeal was unyielding, the journey was laden with hurdles. The traditional mindset of her town found her dreams unconventional and often discouraged her openly. Whispers of skepticism and snickers of disbelief followed her like a shadow, every time she spoke passionately about her latest

learnings or when her eyes lit up while discussing the mysteries of the universe.

In school, her excitement for science was often met with puzzled expressions from her peers. They couldn't grasp the beauty Ada saw in the patterns of nature, the rhythm in the dance of the planets, and the stories written in the stars. They'd giggle when she'd rush to the library during recess instead of the playground, or when she'd choose to spend her weekends at the science club over going to the movies or a picnic.

Some days, the words of her classmates stung. They'd call her 'weird' or 'nerd,' and there were moments when Ada would feel doubt casting a cloud over her dreams. During such times, her mother would cradle

her face, reminding her that it was alright to be different; that her unique perspective was a gift, not a curse. Her father would show her pictures of successful scientists who were once considered odd for their unyielding curiosity and non-conformist dreams.

As Ada continued her small yet significant scientific explorations, there were times when the experiments she eagerly anticipated didn't go as planned. Failed attempts, misunderstood concepts, and unanticipated results sometimes led to frustration. She learned that the path of discovery was not always smooth, but each hurdle was a stepping stone, a lesson leading her closer to understanding the mysteries she so longed to unravel.

As Ada's passion for science blossomed, so did the little science club she had initiated at her school. With her enthusiasm, she was able to kindle a spark of curiosity among her club members, leading them to explore various simple yet intriguing projects. Over time, the club's activities started getting recognition within the local community, and word about their endeavors began to spread.

One bright morning, a local newspaper carried a feature on the young science enthusiasts of the town, with special mention of Ada's enthusiasm and her ability to inspire her peers, despite being just 8 years old. The article highlighted her dream of becoming a scientist and how she had created a mini-haven of curiosity and learning in her backyard.

The story caught the attention of a retired scientist, Dr. Helen Mitchell, who was associated with a prestigious Science Academy for young prodigies. Intrigued and inspired by Ada's story, Dr. Mitchell decided to pay a visit to the young girl whose eyes held the stars.

Arriving in the quaint little town, she met Ada and was thoroughly impressed by the girl's earnest zeal, her grasp of basic scientific concepts, and her unyielding curiosity. Dr. Mitchell spent a day with Ada, observing her interactions with her science club members, her respect for the natural world, and her humble yet persistent approach to seeking knowledge.

Convinced of Ada's potential and inspired by her undeterred spirit, Dr. Mitchell

recommended Ada's name to the Science Academy's special summer program designed to nurture young, promising minds. The academy, upon reviewing Ada's journey so far, her enthusiasm, and her ability to inspire those around her despite societal hurdles, decided to extend an invitation to her to join the program.

It was a fine, breezy morning when Ada received the official letter from the Academy, adorned with its prestigious emblem, acknowledging her passion for science and inviting her to be a part of a community that shared her insatiable thirst for knowledge. As her eyes gleamed with unshed tears of joy, her parents hugged her tight, their hearts swelling with pride for their little girl whose dreams were taking wings, ready to

soar into the vast expanse of endless possibilities.

This story illustrates how genuine passion and a proactive approach, despite young age and societal constraints, can lead you to the future you were always dreaming about.

"The Kind-Hearted Helper"

In a little town named Willowridge, where everyone knew each other's name, there lived an eight-year-old girl named Emily. Emily was known for her bubbly spirit and heart full of kindness. She lived with her

parents and her fluffy cat, Milo, in a cozy blue house with a garden full of colorful flowers. Emily's dad was a firefighter, and her mom was a school teacher. They were a warm and loving family, always ready to lend a helping hand to their neighbors. The town of Willowridge was a friendly and peaceful place where people greeted each other with smiles and open hearts. Emily loved going to school, not only for the education but also to spend time with her friends, especially her best friend, Hannah.

Suddenly, one chilly autumn morning, the peacefulness of Willowridge was shaken when Hannah's house caught fire. Thankfully, everyone was safe, but the house was severely damaged. The news spread like wildfire, and Emily was heartbroken for her

friend. She could see the worry on Hannah's face, and the stress on her parents' faces, too. The challenge was great; Emily felt a deep wish to help, but she didn't know how.

Emily was restless. She would lie awake at night, wondering what she could do to help. She talked to her parents about her feelings, and her mom said, "Emily, even small acts of love can create big waves of joy." But Emily was scared; the task seemed so big for someone so little. However, the more she saw Hannah's sad eyes, the more determined she became.

Emily shared her worry with her teacher, Mrs. Anderson, and her friends at school. They all wanted to help too. Mrs. Anderson suggested they could do something as a

class to help Hannah's family. Ideas buzzed around, but nothing seemed enough until Emily thought of baking.

With a spark of hope, Emily shared her idea of organizing a big bake sale. Everyone loved the idea! They all decided to bake cookies, cupcakes, and other goodies to sell and raise money for Hannah's family. The news spread around Willowridge, and soon enough, the whole town was buzzing with excitement for the Heartfelt Bake.

Emily, her friends, her parents, and even some kind-hearted townsfolk spent days baking. The aroma of fresh-baked goods filled the air, and the morning of the bake sale dawned bright and clear. People from all over came to buy the delicious treats, and

the sense of community was as warm as the sun shining down.

They had raised a generous amount of money by the end of the day. The sight of Hannah's joyful tears and her parents' grateful smiles was the most beautiful scene. Emily felt a warmth in her heart she had never felt before. She learned that even a small act, when done with love and support from others, can make a big difference.

The Heartfelt Bake didn't just help raise money to rebuild a home; it knitted the hearts of the whole community closer. The story of the bake sale became a cherished tale in Willowridge, a sweet reminder of the power of coming together in times of need. Emily now knew that love, mixed with

action, created a recipe for happiness and change. And the joy of giving became a cherished lesson, not just for Emily, but for every heart that beat in the little town of Willowridge.

This story shows how doing kind things for others, with the help of friends and family, can really help someone in need and make everyone feel happy. Emily's idea for a bake sale to help her friend Hannah not only brought money for Hannah's family but also made everyone in town come together like a big happy family. It teaches that even small actions, like baking cookies, when done with love and friends, can make a big, happy difference.

"The Fearless Adventurer"

In a quaint little town named Serene Valley, nestled between rolling hills and sparkling rivers, lived a curious and imaginative girl named Daisy. Daisy had a heart full of dreams but was often tethered by her fears.

She lived in a snug little house with her parents, who were kind and nurturing, always encouraging her to explore her interests. However, venturing into the outdoors, beyond the comforting embrace of her home, was a hurdle she hadn't yet overcome.

Daisy's eyes were like a window to a whimsical world, always daydreaming about the adventures that awaited her beyond her doorstep. But her fears seemed like a tall, invisible wall. Daisy was particularly scared of water, stemming from a small incident when she was younger. So, the idea of outdoor adventures, especially near the rivers, felt like a distant dream.

One sunny day, the local community announced an Outdoor Adventure Camp for

kids to explore and enjoy the natural beauty of Serene Valley. Daisy's heart raced at the thought. This was her chance! She felt a mixture of fear and exhilaration. However, the camp included a small kayaking experience, which immediately sent shivers down Daisy's spine.

Her parents, sensing her hesitation but also her excitement, encouraged her gently to take this step. Her best friend, Ella, also decided to join, which gave Daisy a sliver of hope that she could face her fears.

As the day approached, the butterflies in Daisy's stomach fluttered more and more. The sun on the morning of the adventure day rose bright and clear. Daisy's heart thudded against her chest as she stood at

the edge of the water, the kayak waiting for her. Her parents were there, smiles on their faces but anxiety in their eyes. Ella held her hand, promising to be right beside her.

With a deep breath, Daisy stepped into the kayak, her legs shaking slightly. As the kayak wobbled, her fear skyrocketed, but Ella's reassuring presence and the calm, encouraging words of the instructor helped her steady herself. Each paddle against the gentle water made her heart grow bolder.

She felt the wind in her hair, the cool spray of water on her face, and an unspeakable joy bubbling within. The serene nature, the chirping birds, and the laughter of her mates became a melody she'd never forget.

As Daisy stepped ashore, a mixed whirl of emotions enveloped her. She was the same girl, yet there was a streak of bravery in her now that hadn't been there before. The loud cheer from her parents and friends resonated within her, igniting a tiny spark of self-assurance.

She realized, as she stood there with water droplets trickling down her face, that she had taken her first significant step toward facing her fears. The river that once seemed terrifying was now a symbol of her courage. The smile on her face was gentle, yet carried a depth of understanding that fears could be met with a hopeful heart and tackled, one paddle at a time.

As days turned into nights and then into days again, Daisy found herself reminiscing about her adventure. Everything out there still felt quite daunting, but now she had tasted the essence of self-assurance. The adventure had sowed a seed of courage in her heart, which promised to grow with each passing day. And while she still felt the flutter of fear now and then, Daisy knew she had embarked on a journey of brave exploration, where each step, no matter how shaky, was a step towards a bolder heart and a vivacious spirit.

Her story echoed through Serene Valley School, inspiring other kids to embrace their fears, however big or small. Daisy had shown that fear was but a notion, and with just a little step, one could unveil a strength they never knew existed.

This story tells us that facing our fears is a big part of growing up and having fun adventures. With help and kind words from family and friends, we can be brave and try new things, even if they seem scary at first. Daisy's story shows that when we take small steps to face our fears, we become braver and help others feel brave too!

Afterword

Dear girl,

Oh, what splendid journeys we've had together through the pages of this magical book! We've danced with brave hearts, soared through skies of self-belief, and discovered hidden treasures of courage.

As we turn this last page together, the magic doesn't end, but continues to twinkle within your heart, ready to shine bright in the adventures that await you. Remember, dear girl, every challenge you face is a chance to sprinkle a little more magic into the world.

The brave girls in these stories left trails of sparkles wherever they danced, and now it's

your turn. Your heart is a garden of endless possibilities, blooming with dreams, courage, and love. And with each step you take, may your unique magic spread joy, hope, and a sprinkle of dream-dust around.

Our tales may have paused for now, but your story is just beginning to twirl into the endless dance of life. With a heart full of dreams and a sprinkle of courage, there's no star too far to reach.

As you close this book, take with you the melodies of bravery, the rhythm of self-love, and the tunes of self-confidence. Dance to them, laugh with them, and share them with the world. For you are a remarkable story, continuing to be written with every beat of your brave heart.

The world is a better place with your unique sparkle in it.

Keep shining, dreaming, and being the amazing you!

Made in the USA
Las Vegas, NV
21 November 2023

81183374R10049